To Pennie – Jacob
For my teachers and my students – K-Fai

www.enchantedlion.com

First edition published in 2020 by Enchanted Lion Books
67 West Street, Suite 403, Brooklyn, New York 11222
Text © 2020 by Jacob Kramer
Illustrations © 2020 by K-Fai Steele
All rights reserved under International and Pan-American Copyright Conventions
A CIP record is on file with the Library of Congress
Printed in China by RR Donnelley Asia Printing Solutions Ltd.
ISBN: 978-1-59270-304-3
First Printing

Jacob Kramer

K-Fai Steele

Okapi
Tale

Enchanted Lion Books

NEW YORK

Not so long ago, Noodlephant and her friends invented a machine that would turn anything into noodles.

Using the Phantastic Noodler,
they turned pillows into *ravioli* and
shoelaces into *spaghetti*. It was such
a wonderful machine, they gave it
to the town for all to use.

Animals from far and wide flocked to Beaston to crank stuff through the machine.
Noodlephant's friends welcomed the newcomers and invited them to picnic together.

But not everyone in Beaston was happy. The kangaroos missed the days when the town was called "Rooville," and they were the only ones in charge. They grumbled and whined about their new neighbors. They even complained to the Mayor.

Noodlephant was so inspired by all the visitors that she now wanted to travel the world. She took a job as a cook on a ship sailing to Japan and China, places famous for their noodles.

As Noodlephant was boarding, an Okapi disembarked.

"Enjoy Beaston!" called Noodlephant, but the Okapi just sniffed his snooty snout.

"Don't mind that Okapi-talist," said the Captain, "He's very rude, and only cares about money."

As soon as the Okapi saw the Phantastic Noodler, he wanted to buy it.

"Who owns this machine?" asked the Okapi.

"Nobody," said the Fly, "It's public! That means it belongs to everyone."

"Someone must own it," declared the Okapi. "*Everything* belongs to someone."

The Mice—who had lovely voices—burst into song:

We built this machine together.
It's for everybody to use.
Whether you're scaly, or hairy, or feathered
There's noodles for me's and for you's!

When everyone owns it, nobody does
We can share all the things we produce.
Whether you're covered in spines or in fuzz
There's noodles for me's and for you's!

The Okapi snorted and went
to see the Mayor.

"I'd like to buy your old machine," said the Okapi. "It's dented and clutters up the park. Besides, it's attracting all kinds of vermin."

The Mayor nodded, "These newcomers are ruining Rooville."

"Sell it to me," said the Okapi. "I'll help you restore the good old days."

The Okapi wrote the Mayor a big check,
and they sealed the deal.

The next morning, when the animals of Beaston went to make noodles, all they found was a sign:

MEANWHILE, Noodlephant was enjoying Japan, a place famous for *udon*, *soba*, and *ramen*. One day, Noodlephant found herself in the middle of a parade of dancers wearing tall wooden clogs called *geta*. They looked like so much fun!

Noodlephant bought an extra-extra large pair for herself, and matching sets for her friends.

But back home, unbeknownst to Noodlephant …

… things were getting much, much worse.

The Okapi's factory had turned all beach shells into *conchiglie* and the leaves into *foglie*. One day, the butterflies vanished from the butterfly garden, and the next night, boxes of *farfalle* were being loaded onto trucks.

With all the money he was making, the Okapi bought up the town.
He bought the grocery store, the Beastro, and the farmer's market.
Each time, he raised the prices to get more money.

The only way Noodlephant's friends could get enough money to buy food was to work in the Okapi's factory.

Day by day, the Okapi ordered them to work faster and faster, cranking out more and more pasta.

The workers protested outside City Hall, but the Mayor just shrugged.

"Job creators like the Okapi are beautifying Rooville and making it safer. Look at these statues, and the shiny new cages in the Zoo!"

Noodlephant's friends chanted:

Cages cannot make us safer
Statues cannot feed our town!
The bad old days won't be our future
We demand that you step down!

"How dare you speak to a
kangaroo like that!" snapped
the Mayor. He went inside
to meet with the Okapi.

MEANWHILE, Noodlephant was having a great time in China.

She learned to stretch *biang biang* and eat them with spicy chili sauce. She loved slurping floppy sheets of *pu gai mian*.

But one day, Noodlephant saw a strange new brand of pasta at the market.

Holding the box, her trunk tingled with fear. Deep down, she knew something had gone very, very wrong.

Noodlephant rushed to the docks, where her shipmates were loading crates of juicy peaches.

"My friends need me at home, in Beaston," she told the Captain. "Can you help?"

"Of course! We sail tonight!"

At sea, Noodlephant cooked and sang with her shipmates.

The more I see, the more I think
About how we can change our ways
To share in common all the things
That help us live throughout our days:

Food and water, medicines
Hot tubs, energy, and trains
Housing and the wilderness
Factories for making things

Orchards, farms and neighborhoods
Are not for the wealthy few
They should be held as public goods
They all belong to me and you!

A few weeks later, Noodlephant arrived home. Her friends rushed to meet her at the dock.
They hugged, ate peaches and opened their presents. Everyone *clip-clopped* on their new *geta*.
They stayed up late into the night, making plans.

The next morning at the factory,
everyone was a little bit taller and a little bit wobbly.

When the work whistle blew, they began to work, but slooowly.
After an hour, they had only turned one bell into a single *campanello*.

"Where's my pasta?" demanded the Okapi. "We need to ship 3,000 boxes by midnight!"

The workers began to move even slower.

"Move, you lazy sloths! Work! Work faster!" shouted the Okapi.

Slooowly, Noodlephant raised her trunk.

The signal! In a flash, the workers jammed
their *geta* into the Phantastic Noodler.
The machine shook, sputtered,
and oozed thick stinking goo.
It was completely *clogged*!

The workers declared:

With all due respect, Mr. Okapi
We've had quite enough of your greed!
You're selfish and mean, controlling and bossy
You've taken much more than you need.

We are entitled to all we've created
Including this noodle machine.
We're taking it back, we will not be cheated
We're no longer part of your scheme.

"I bought it fair and square!" cried the Okapi.

"The Mayor had no right to sell it," said the Fly,
"It belongs to all of us."

"But I *own* it!" whined the Okapi.

"Let's settle this," said Noodlephant, "with a vote."

Soon, all of Beaston was gathered to vote on the question:

When the votes were counted, the majority agreed:
The machine was a public good and could not be
privately owned.

The next day, the workers brought crates of juicy peaches to City Hall, *impeached* the Mayor, and sent him packing.

Soon, Beaston elected a new Mayor …
someone who would do a *fly-tastic* job.

For the inauguration,
Noodlephant cranked
blankets through the
Noodler, making loads
of floppy *pu gai mian*.

And the mice, of course, led the chorus:

We are making decisions together
For the many! Not just the few.
Whether you're scaly or hairy or feathered
Democracy's for me's and you's!

When nobody owns things, everyone does
We can share everything that we use
Whether you're covered in spines or in fuzz
Democracy's for me's and you's!

As for the Okapitalist, he had trouble making money in Beaston. Nobody would shop at his stores, or even talk to him. So, he picked up and left town.

Who knows … maybe he's headed your way.